How to get out of an
Unemployment Trap

Khushbu Jain

RG
books

Published By

Redgrab Books Pvt. Ltd.

942, Mutthiganj, Prayagraj, 211003

www.redgrabbooks.com

contact@redgrabbooks.com

Price in india : 225/- INR

First published by Redgrab Books in 2023
Copyright © 2023 Redgrab Books Pvt. Ltd.
Copyright Text © 2023 Khushbu Jain
Printed and bound in India
Cover Design & Typesetting by Redgrab Books team
ISBN : 978-93-95697-16-3

DEDICATION

This book is about hope, and I'd like to dedicate it to the people in my community who daydream or nightdream. I also want to dedicate this book to the unemployed of our nation.

BOOK SUMMARY

It is a book regarding the problems that unemployed people face in their corporate life. Things before lockdown are different from things after lockdown. However, the impact on employees was much greater after the lockdown.

Many of the employees faced rejection, many of the employees got fired in the middle of their careers, and they are still struggling for a regular income source. And with due respect to such talented candidates, I have thought to share some important points regarding their career growth and money-making with them. And also, I would like to deliver some positive thoughts, as they required emotional support too.

This book is for hope. This book is to make professional people aware of the environment of the company. Also, what challenges do candidates face before entering a corporate job?

Some ex-employees have no idea about their abilities because they have devoted their entire lives to the corporate companies that fired them during the lockdowns. And after the lockdown, these people were facing more problems due to their whole soul's dedication to the same work for a long period. Why does a company require a bond signatory from a candidate to work with them for a longer period? But any employee ever dared to ask them to sign the bond for a job guarantee. Currently, employees are facing a problem of making monthly early which is not like in previous life to ask for a hike in corporate life.

Why does Women's Unemployment Increase? Why they can't work in a good environment? Why is there a gap between employees, colleagues, and seniors in understanding the path? Why do students want to go abroad for higher studies and higher growth in their careers? Why is our education system not merely good as compared to countries like the USA? What ability does the unemployed have inside them?

These things are explained by the author with a real-life-based example for readers to understand better.

ACKNOWLEDGEMENT

Before turning this page and start reading the Book ''How to get out of an Unemployment Trap" I would like to express my gratitude towards my parents, my teacher, and my brother Jogesh Jain who always supported me and gave importance to my decisions, by which I was able to make a change in my life and also going to make a change in this world by this book.

I decided to write this book at the beginning of 2020 with the intention of spreading positivity to people in the early years through my philosophical thoughts and also as a failed student and a passionate person to achieve her dream.

I completed only fifty percent of the work in this book when the lockdown arose. Looking at the situation, my confidence level increased for completing the remaining book, knowing that I am on the right path. I worked harder till I completed this book.

I had no idea that lockdown would cause such a huge loss in the professional field, and that it would effectively increase in future decades if no one ever found a solution. In this world, we need to live together and tackle the situation together. We also need to overcome the loss together to receive good returns.

Being a struggler for more than two or three years, being a motivational hustler, and also being an artist, I wrote this book. I am not a guide liner for you, I am not an expert, but I am the writer, and I wrote this based on my observation. Somewhat real experience, and also learning things from individual people.

CONTENT

Introduction: The worst day of my life.   11

Chapter 1

Fresher's diagonal   17

Something about your dream   18

Change your mindset   18

Dream job   19

Over/lower confidence   21

Flexibility   22

Chapter-2

Unemployability   23

What does unemployment mean after   24

Game-changing decision   26

How did the unemployed give their interview?   28

Everyone has their own story   30

Types of unemployment   31

Selection and Rejection   32

Chapter-3

Unemployment ability   35

Chapter-4

Women's unemployment   37

Financially secure yourself   37

Generation gap   38

Judgemental decision-making   38

Self-growth   39

Update yourself   39

Chapter-5

Employees risk segmentation   40

Communication   44

Women's Unemployability 46

Find your uniqueness 51

Chapter-6

Business Development plans 54

Timing of our success 59

Progress report 59

Chapter -7

Education-based career opportunity 62

What if a second lockdown will arrive 64

Chapter-8

Self Development 67

Talk to self 67

Share your disability 68

Concentration 69

Self believe 70

Chapter-9

Positive Affirmations 71

Celebrate failure 72

Learn from mistakes 73

Commitment to self 75

Chapter-10

Revolutionary 77

Trust yourself 79

Do what you want to do 81

Mental Health must be good 82

Conclusion 84

INTRODUCTION

The worst day of my life

I got rejection at the beginning of my career. After rejection at the beginning itself, I lost confidence that it was me who had lost passion for life and lost passion for getting a job at the start of my career.

In the year 2019, I was a newly graduated person with a bachelor's degree in commerce and thought I would go to a new city for a job. This was the age where you had an inbuilt passion to do something in life.

As one might expect, the failures on their way to success.

It was my 1st ever interview as I expected it to happen. I wanted to work in an MNC and build a good career for the rest of my life. But it is not so easy or difficult when your vision is clear.

The company is based in Germany and is a very well-known body of private-sector accounting. As a result, it is clear that to be a good accountant, you must have good knowledge, learning preferences, and better career goals. I was confident in the company where I would work because I believed it had the potential to succeed.

Let's talk about the interview day overview. I received a call from the HR consultancy regarding the job. He had fixed my interview on the same day, and I went for a f2f interview at the company location. I did not have lunch and had no time to prepare anything for the interview. I had to go early by bus to reach the office location on time. Because I had to change 2 buses from my location to the office location, the first thing that came to mind was to arrive on time for the interview to demonstrate that you are a punctual and time-management employee. Because I have seen and learned from the corporate environment that your first impression is your last impression.

But can you tell me, can you make a business decision in the first meeting or with just one phone call? You must have the time and patience to make an important decision. Similarly, you must give people time to understand and determine the compatibility of that person. At the very least, keep the second impression in mind.

I arrived on time and waited for half an hour to find out who is the interviewer. I was searching the company website for previous achievements and decided that I had to work for this company only. While going to the interview room, I started imagining everything, like what would be my desk, our discussion room, and who would be my TL. This is not my overconfidence, but it's a way to boost confidence within.

I have no idea how to talk to the interviewer. I was waiting for Madam, who was going to take my interview.

She asked me a few general questions, starting with "Introduce yourself."

I gave her answer in a very short way, that my name is Khushbu Jain, and my graduation is BCom. About my ongoing course information: I am preparing for a competitive exam and, coming to my hobbies, I like to write poems. I wrote around 20 poems, and a few of them were published (currently I have a published book). I also like to travel, listen to music, and play chess. (I dislike being told anything about myself.)

She told me to wait for some time. The next round will begin in a few minutes, so be ready for it.

The next round of interviews began, with one sir and ma'am with whom I had completed my first round of interviews. They had started asking accounting questions. They asked me about the 3 golden rules of accounting; what is debit or credit; journal entries, etc. I was able to give all the answers because at that time I was a fresh graduate. My confidence was very low. As in the human body, haemoglobin deficiency generates the same thing as me with no confidence.

   How to get out of an Unemployment Trap

Interviewer: Tell me about VAT tax and the taxation rate associated with products. Whatever I remembered, I answered, but I was not sure about it.

I: Did you ever do online shopping? You should get the idea of a bill with a deduction rate.

Did you ever go for dinner in a restaurant and also find a bill?

My answer is against them that I never gave anyone treats in restaurants, but yes, I went alone to eat in restaurants.

They laughed and cracked jokes at my answer.

After some time, they realize why is there this nervousness, because this is my first interview. Now, they tried to check my skills as well as my confidence level by asking, if I got selected for the next round. We have a chess player in our office, and we would like to see the match between the two champions. If you win, the job is yours. I am happy that I got a chance to play chess. Later I was informed that the chess match is postponed.

They asked me to write down one poem on the company's laptop and read it out loud. Nobody knows whether the interviewer wants to hear your talent or if he is only interested in testing your mental capacity.

They both told me to take a lunch break till 2 pm. After that, your 3rd round will be scheduled, so prepare yourself for the next round. (I thought that they will ask me to leave and never come again).

Before I left, Mam gave me some tips on how to communicate in front of the sir who would be conducting my next round of interviews. He is strict, if he finds any mistakes, you will get rejected. Try to introduce yourself very well and speak a little bit louder with confidence. I was not able to take food under stress, but I have to take it for fresh energy to give a good interview.

In the interview room, I was waiting, and suddenly one

man came with specs on his face. He looked very sincere and silent. I found an accurate imagination of those people who were very silent. Their violence is very dangerous. I found another sir also sitting on the opposite side of the desk doing something on the computer, and he was watching me for help because he had taken my second-round interview. The sincere man in front of me asked me to introduce myself. While I was giving my introduction this time properly, with no hurry, he was putting a watch on me. After giving the interview, they told me that they would inform HR if they wanted to hire me. You may leave.

Now, it's time to get feedback from HR to know whether I have a chance to get that job.

While I was out, I crossed the surface and went in the opposite direction of the office from where I had to go back to the bus stop. I was finding my way to walk. That time, without wasting much time, I called HR and gave him the information regarding a job.

*This is a very important point that every candidate has to keep in mind. You have to explain every single point of your interview in detail to the HR because he/she is the one who understands your path, who knows your strengths and weaknesses. They are the ones who speak from your side to the company. I have given all the information; good path, bad path, where I lost confidence, and my negative things; he told me that they will understand; don't worry, and I can speak up with them once when I take feedback. He told me that he will call me back soon.

After 15 minutes, HR called me back and said that up till now I got the idea that your overall interview was good, just a little bit. You have to increase your confidence and they will like your knowledge of the job, you have to be patient till you get hired.

One more thing I want to add to this is that companies

    How to get out of an Unemployment Trap

have many candidate options. Some are freshers like me, who want to start a career, and some are experienced, they are always in demand. This is tough competition between fresh and experienced candidates, and the problem is that only one position is guaranteed. The guess who will get this position is the experienced candidate.

Regarding my knowledge: I don't have much, but I have enough to get started.

About my skills: I am a newcomer who had never worked before.

• About Experience: As I didn't get the opportunity to work, I have no experience.

• About Confidence: -Till now I have not achieved anything or perfection in work.

This is the scenario of my interview, where I wanted only one chance to start my career journey, but it didn't happen.

After 2 days, I received a call at 2 pm from the same company, asking me to in 1 hr to their office. Without wasting time, I immediately went out. I felt curious about the question, "Why did they call me?" I reached the office within one hour. After waiting for half an hour, they gave me directions to go inside the door on the right side of the table. A few people remember me, and the smiles on their faces make me positive.

I found one man who was senior in age and possession in the company. He was very focused on the PC. The first question, he asked for the resume, which I did not forget, but had no money to print out. I told him that my resume is in the office, or if you want, I can mail it to you. He said there was no need and that I should make a note of it.

He asked me to give a brief introduction about myself, and whatever I told him about my name, education, family background, and skills, I stated unquestionably that whatever courses I had taken, I never had the opportunity to work on them. As well, I don't have a PC. After a few minutes that Sr. Sir said goodbye to me.

This day became the worst for me.

They never asked or said that they were looking for an experienced candidate. Again, I called HR, he told me that they had selected another candidate.

What exactly does an interviewer want from you?

Chapter-1
FRESHER'S DIAGONAL

With my real-life example, I have divided this topic into 3 different parts.

Opportunity missed for a Career: It's mutually connected with my previous example of the MNC company interview.

But I have another thing to share with my readers.

When I used to find a good job for myself, I desperately went straight to ask for an appointment.

I came across a CA firm near my place. I thought to give it a try, I went to the first floor of the society. The girl receptionist told me to wait for some time. I thought she was strict or what? I saw that everyone was working silently. Two men were discussing work on a PC. I found it could be a productive opportunity for me to work with seniors in a professional environment.

It's time to go for the interview. I had a good interview with full confidence, your eye contact, and valuable conversation must give a good impact on their mindset to change for you. The very next day, he called me to meet. I went there, and this time he was attentive towards me, he told me that; I was working, and suddenly I thought of your resume and thought to call you.

I was getting confused about planning for a PG degree. I have planned that I can check for a decent-paid job to pay for my degree. I am not ready to take out education loans at that time.

I want to go join a CA firm that pays me 10K per month, but my confidence is not allowing me due to my first rejection, that's the mistake I have made, and want to share it with my youngest readers to learn from it. This impact affected my career, and I didn't accept their proposal.

I joined one HR consultancy. I was playing the role of HR with some different responsibilities; my readers should have an idea of HR work. The consultancy was closed down within a month. I didn't find any way to go back to the CA firm and ask for the job. My anxiety spoke louder than my present situation. This story was before COVID-19.

Something about your dream:

Attitude is something that consoles your lifestyle. You must keep a positive attitude, which describes your personality. Don't forget to show the real you, which is not known at the corporate office.

If you are going for an interview with multiple corporate companies, they will judge you by every single way you react, walk, or talk. So, it's better to do nothing than to do something like a task that you're comfortable with; all you have to do is give them clarity on what you can do because everyone has their versions.

Before getting a job, you must tell them about your weaknesses. You do not need to hide because, as a human being, everyone has their weakest point and darkest story inside. By this, you may also get the impression that the company cares for you. By this, they might consider your work preferences. After all, you are considered the company's assets. Try your best to make your valuable resources.

Change your mindset.

''Attitude in positive efforts is good.''

Suppose one person went to an IT company for a job interview. He developed and mentioned some skills related to the job position. To divert the interviewer's attention, the candidate changes their choices and interests and makes

          How to get out of an Unemployment Trap

themselves available to fulfill all such requirements by becoming robots. This is not the right way to get the job. By doing this, many companies change their patterns, creating tough competition in the market.

If you are interested in working, it's alright, but if you are looking forward to showing that you are not from the same background and doing it well, that's not a good attitude. This type of candidate is only money-oriented, they work as per their needs and requirements and then leave.

As a result of this situation, many deserving/needy candidates do not get the opportunity. This is the main reason that in corporate sectors, the biggest battle takes place between job seekers and experienced employees. But some unemployed employees who were not getting any job in their firm were working on developing other skills to get that particular job, which became beneficial to them.

However, don't judge a story by its title. - Khushbu Jain

Dream Job

A dream job is nothing but work that gives you happiness, money, and peace. For this, many of us work on developing skills, paying more and more attention to them, and also enjoyed learning about them. Some of my readers' dream jobs will pay them more money, and some will pay less. But in both conditions, one thing is clear, i.e., peace. It's as if some have had love marriages and others have had arranged marriages, but the most important thing is that they had different experiences, such as some having great benefits and others having fewer benefits, and I can't guarantee peace in it.

Did you ever see or find your dream job in a minute or second in your hand? Let me tell you about a coach, author, and founder of JJSE, i.e., Jogesh Jain School of Employability. The man who is chasing his dream in real life. Many employees and graduate students are in his network and are taking guidance from him to get their dream job. How to get that job book written by him to guide you towards your career.

Let me tell you about one of his student achievements with a great message.

On April 21, 2021, I received a WhatsApp message from a person asking for the guidelines for launching his book on Amazon KDP. I asked him for all the details regarding the book and its status of the book. We have decided on a fixed time to talk on the call, and I am going to explain to him all the things like how to describe a book, title, cover, secret of the kdp policy, royalties, etc. Our conversation was in English most of the time, but sometimes in Hindi as well, but the thing is, our communication was very helpful, understandable, and productive. This is the actual point I want to explain to my readers.

The conversation is not about you talking in a professional language, i.e., English. That's only compulsory in India to show off or to stay in a professional environment, but here it is important to have some productive talk that is in use of your work.

Let me share with you one more real example of a Linkedin person.

He is a Punjabi man, a poet, an author, and a motivational influencer who went for a job interview at one of the MNCs. He requested them to take his interview in the Hindi language, with which he is comfortable. The interview is done. He has explained his skills and work experience. They were impressed and gave him the job.

Many of the comments I read on his post said that someone was talking positively about English and in India, the most spoken language is English rather than the mother tongue of which we should be proud. We are still facing problems.

   How to get out of an Unemployment Trap

Language should never be a barrier in any work field, work doesn't permit language learning; it has to be completed, never needed to know how.

Some people thought that this happened by chance. In many of those cases, the candidates get rejected.

I want to convey that, whether it happened by luck or not, corporate sectors should think about a change and give a chance to the talented ones.

Let me ask why Prime Minister Modi Sir gives speeches in Hindi all over the world; sometimes he speaks in English, but mostly he only speaks in Hindi.

Option A: He is not fluent in English.

Option B: He is proud of his native language.

Who has made this rule in India? To talk and give interviews only in English.

Option A: Mahatma Gandhi,

Option B: Interviewers

Option C: Corporate offices Extreme self-assurance

Over/Lower Confidence

It's human nature, but we need to know when to show and when not to.

When a person lies, he or she must imitate with overconfidence, and when a person speaks the truth, he or she must have low confidence.

It's a fact, I am not saying anything new. This kind of thing happens in our lives from childhood. Because we don't have the habit of telling the truth all the time. It's normal to lie for little things like skipping classes for fun.

So my question is to company interviewers: are you interested in truthful people who are trustworthy and who will be loyal to your company, or are you willing to take a lier into your company who will be a temporary part of your company? When you take an interview with a candidate who is shy, fearful, or low-confidence, here you will find an intense candidate who is loyal to you and your company, so don't judge your candidate. Their performance must not affect it.

But, your confidence in the candidates must be the best investment for that candidate.

Flexibility

Freshers have that kind of flexibility if they decide to work hard and if they set goals. But something is missing in their lives, i.e., career guidelines. Here they make a mistake. They preferred a career counsellor, but they didn't think to ask themselves. They have low confidence in themselves.

Tell me one thing: who knows you better?

Option A is you, and Option B is something else.

They must guide you, but they tell you to purchase their courses. Students' investment is higher as compared to any other investor because to get a good job they have to pay fees. If they want the best degree just to show on their resume, they have to pay money. What happens if a student is still facing problems and is struggling to get a job then?

One wants you to think about it. What should our upcoming junior new generation think about us? What will they learn from you?

    How to get out of an Unemployment Trap

Chapter-2
UNEMPLOYABILITY

We have all seen unemployment problems all over the world. Previously, India was known for its population growth, but now one more name has been added, i.e., unemployment growth. Not only for the Indian people, but we were not taking care of our country's people. During the lockdown, such companies deal with losses, and due to that, many employees get fired from their jobs permanently. But I just want to ask one thing: what does a company guarantee when you perform well, they have no guarantee of you because they just want their work should be done on time, no matter what it takes.

Many of the employees who worked with dedication for the company and even the oldest employees get fired. Many of the employees are dependent on their jobs, but still, they get fired. It is not fair for them.

Don't love your company.

Love your job. —Unknown

People generally know everything, but some of them ignore reality like "seen but not reacted to," "helping nature," and "pray for better reach, "this thing happened on LinkedIn."

Many such employees are now unemployed, and their degrees, experience, and everything else has been wasted. If they want a job in any other field, they have to adjust to less salary, and currently, to fulfil their family needs, they require more money. In their field, they face a struggle to get a job because of the constant competition no matter who organizes it but to get a job, you have to give tough competition in the market.

They are dealing with some mental stress as well. They see themselves as failures: uneducated, tired, and weak. They are the people who used to be proud to say they worked for a multinational corporation and lived a fashionable lifestyle, but now they act like people in poverty, constantly asking for work, a job, and money. They are the ones who are proud of their profession; they have settled but are now desperate for work, at any level of the sector, for money, to support their families. We all have to take part in the solution because karma believes in action. My message is to employees, companies, and businesses as an Indian. It's not only the duty of the government, PM Modi, but we all have to try out at least once to rate down unemployability in India.

I just hope this book will be helpful.

What does unemployment mean after Lockdown?

Unemployment may just be like an employee who has not been used by the company at all after giving his precious time with dedication and life to the company for its growth. However, the actual meaning is that employees with low-performance levels are fired from the company.

Everyone has their way of learning and achieving goals.

The problem of unemployment has become very vast after the increase in India's population, as compared to urban jobless lockdowns. COVID-19 Previously, India was facing a poverty problem, but now the country's income doesn't fulfil the needs of its people. They were trying to get money through their efforts, but currently, this is affecting the country's funding and settlement.

The lockdown affected human life, corporate companies, and businesses, and this has become a disaster for the whole world.

Try to find some of the answers to my questions on your own or from this book.

1. Why do MNC companies fire many of their employees? even if they perform with perfection.

How to get out of an Unemployment Trap

2. Why does a company reject you?

3. What drew you to your previous job?

4. Why is India facing problems with the economy?

5. Why do people want to be their own boss in a firm?

I have seen candidates struggle apart from the professional area. They are first in contact with HR consultancy and some of the consultancy firms in India are taking advantage of those candidates' helplessness. They take the money and say it is refundable, but no, they never write to you.

Let me tell you how they work with my experience.

One day, I went to my local mall sector. In that mall, many of the private companies offices are located. I was roaming around trying to find an event management company, but I didn't find any. I went there to get a better understanding and asked for a job placement. Two people talked with me as a counsellor and shared tips for cracking jobs and getting placements. They have set offers for different fields of work. As they told me; as a fresher, you have a very low chances of getting a job, but if you trust us, we will give you a job of your choice in your area with a good salary package and good timing. We have the option that if you want to be in BPO, there is a very small amount to pay before the 1st round of interviews, which will happen in our consultancy. I remembered the rate, but for the account, he told me to pay around 10,000 because we are helping you to get a good job.

Try to close this type of consultancy in India. This is an illegal business.

Let me share with you one more example of consultancy. It's a real-life example.

One of my friends went to the consultancy in Pune at Yerwada for a job. They offered him and 15 other candidates with the same details about the job description and salary package. They all gave their 1st round of interviews with that consultancy holder, a well-known educator, with just a small introduction. We were all waiting for the next interview because they said that the IT companies' HR was coming to take our interview. After sometime before 15 minutes, they gave actual information about the company's policies, like for rotational shifts. Yes, yes, for overtime. Yes, if your salary is less than that. I'm requesting a negotiation.

Whatever they ask, just say yes, even if the candidate has a problem. They promised that when you are on board, we will change something for you. The consultancy received a commission from the IT sector to place such a candidate with their company, but the candidate still struggled. This is also illegal. Many of the candidates are directly contacting the company via website, mail, or contact number for jobs. My request to companies is to accept such a call and, if you like the candidate's potential, give him/her one chance.

Why are many MNC companies posting difficult challenges by making their policies unfavorable to candidates?

Many private companies are asking for experience from candidates over their age, where they will find experience. Nowadays, it doesn't matter to them but matters to those candidates.

At least before setting your requirements and job policy, keep a check on those candidates' educational backgrounds for the job.

Game-changing decisions

Before starting anything new, I would like to share one story.

The story of a client and a dedicated candidate

When I was working in human resources consulting, I used to select candidates as per the requirements.

Client Requirements

          How to get out of an Unemployment Trap

Job description

Job position: Lead Generation

Experience (3 to 5 yrs.)

Education: Graduation in any field.

Skills: fluent communication in English, verbal, confidential experience, knowledge, punctuality, and all those responsibilities that the client mentioned in his JD.

All of those responsibilities are well-known to the candidate due to his many years of experience in this field, and he is an expert candidate.

On the present day, I gave him a call and confirmed that if he was interested, I gave him the address to reach on time for the interview on the very next day. My candidate was half an hour late due to the rainy day because he couldn't find a bus. Somehow, he managed to get to the interview.

I received a call from the client whose requirements I was going to fulfill that day. But it hasn't happened. He was angry, shouting on the call that what kind of candidate you were sending for the interview, he did not know how to behave in an interview. If you are unable to do this work, I will find someone else's consultancy.

I was very polite to him. I tried hard to convince him and change his decision, by explaining to him the positive qualities of the candidate's profile, his skills, experience, and everything I was able to do. (Don't think sympathetically, but it's an HR duty to provide a punctual candidate for a job. It's professional.) He is trustworthy and knows his candidate very well because of their first conversation, which directly converted them into believers. This HR inquired about you, your skills, and your dedication to assisting you, as this HR knows the candidate very well. Aside from the client, whose point of view is unclear,

After that call, I immediately called my candidate, asking him everything about the interview. How did you give your interview? I asked him in a normal way. He said that I explained to him my work, skills, achievements, and knowledge. I gave all the answers properly.

I asked him what the reason for your rejection was then. He told me that he disliked my attitude (in a positive way). He was looking for a reason to reject me due to his ego. Because of our communication gap, which is the reason he disliked and rejected me.

I cross-checked with my boss through a call and asked for feedback from that Clint. He gave communication results and expected a more varied set of candidates. He was looking for the best English speaker for the job.

This was the reason I thought of writing a book on unemployment (2 years back). In this world, no one is perfect. Because God knows if he makes perfect humans, they will show attitude and disrespect to others.

It's not important to be perfect in everything, but you have that perfection skill, which is mandatory for all.

"Perfection must be in performance, not in results." Jain, Khushbu

Some of the decisions damage the candidates' careers for sure.

Try to speak up in your upcoming interviews about this type of rejection from the previous company.

How did the unemployed give his interview?

-He will share his previous rejection story with the interviewer.

-He will share the list of weaknesses in him.

Why? "Because you are scared of the rejection." They will judge you based on your previous rejections. right?

If you don't speak up to them like in my candidate story, that kind of client will not stop doing these things.

 How to get out of an Unemployment Trap

-Bad experiences come from the worst situations, and bad experiences take place after you step forward.

Worst day, the worst experience, the hungry mind is enough to get back up. — Jain Khushbu.

Companies have to start checking their employees' skills for bad experiences so that they may get an idea of how to perform under pressure and how to tackle those situations in their professional life. Because corporate sector employees needed risk-taking decisions to solve such decades in businesses,

Why did I get the job? Why was I let go?

Your hobby must be your profession, or not?

"Passion automatically splits into professions."

"Your hobby becomes your profession," and also, your hobby is just different from your profession to make your career. Because that degree is not as important as the profession, in addition, if you are moving on to such a profession, you will require higher qualifications to settle for a job and achieve that profession.

My point in this is that, firstly, this is about your hobby, in which no means of graduation is required. Anything you want to put in there, don't change it because of some stupid question mark from society. Many artists give up their passion to make it a profession due to social disconfirmation and because it's not on the list of professions. In your parents' eyes.

Maintain your confidence in your ability to win.

Many of my readers have heard of this hobby in their group, i.e., men doing belly dance. This is an excellent example of pushing your dream past its boundaries. I've read in many of their stories that they faced very difficult challenges in their lives, such as being hurt by their parents, family feuds, and financial difficulties. But the only thing is that they never stop believing in their decision to succeed.

No one will help you out until you help yourself.

Whoever does not help himself will never help others.

Another Profession-Related Example

I read this thing earlier. An employee of LinkedIn provided the example.

He wrote that I liked to play guitar, but I have no time to do this type of activity in life. I sometimes forget how much I enjoy playing the guitar. I was tired and bored with my daily routines. I realized that I needed to remain tense to become stress-free in music, so I started practicing guitar at home. He felt better after this activity and decided to take some time from the daily routine to do the things he chooses in life. This was the balancing of your personal and professional choices. Don't forget that you have natural resources inside you. Many of these platforms are online, like Facebook and YouTube, where you may share your skills and thoughts with them.

We all have options to decide on anything, and we get confused about the actual choices to be made. Everyone has their dream, choice, and many things, so don't get confused about them. Keep your personal and professional choices different and use them at work.

You may give online classes. You might have thought that you are not a professional guitarist, but after some attempts, you will get to be that expert. This is a small thing for others, but you can set your own choices as well.

Everyone has their own story.

I will tell you one unseen story.

He knows he can't tell them, but he also knows he can't live with lies.

One anxious candidate went for the interview and was rejected because he was bad at presentation and was not able to present himself in front of Clint. He always makes the same mistakes, but his efforts never make him stop. He had attempted 100 job interviews up to this point.

Interviewers only value working professionals. He had no choice but to get up. Because companies hire you to work for them according to their directions only, and if you do not give them satisfactory performance, they will not accept you.

But companies don't allow a candidate who is facing problems, and that is also correct for them if they are dealing with losses.

Many such candidates deal with stress and anxiety since they miss their career growth opportunities by themselves.

The solution is to try to survive alone in that position.

Types of unemployment.

• The oldest – has less energy, is less focused on work, is tired, is rigid, has family responsibilities, is a compromised employee, and is loyal.

• Middle – These people have a burning desire to do something, but they haven't had the opportunity, and they sometimes struggle to get out of it. It proves they don't want to impress. They are pure talent.

• Youngest – Excessively energetic, disorganized, and performs following their work style. People underestimate them. Live with a long attitude, never satisfied.

The difference between employment and unemployment is a complete transformation.

As an unemployed person, you have a great deal of time to accomplish your work. You have the flexibility quality that an employed person has but is unable to work due to lack of time. From the youngest generation, you must become a quick learner. And in your dedicated nature, you will surely become an experienced person who doesn't know everything all the time but has the planning to change strategy and has faced many things in life.

Selection and Rejection

In 2021, companies will open with job requirements in the market. Those days are hard to predict market demand for. Everyone wants to earn money, keep money secure and work hard. The candidates didn't know whether they were getting a job or not. And employees were tense about whose number was next to be fired from the office.

I was in my hometown, I am trying hard to get a job. During the lockdown, I developed my writing skills and learned new things. I received a direct call from the company's HR for a content writing job. "I didn't react until I got the confirmation." I targeted those companies, where I knew, I could easily get to work. And, I had to give 2 rounds of interviews for the selection and one more later for the job confirmation.

I passed my written test, which was set for me to write, and I was happy at that time because I have the chance to get this job.

The second round will be a video call with the senior mam of the office. In this round, I have to give a brief introduction as well, they will tell me my responsibilities, work, and everything else, just like a simple small induction into the company. Our conversation is much more progressive and impressive to persuade for the job. She informed me that we are looking for long-term employees and that if you are hired, we will have to teach you everything. I said yes, I am OK with that. I am OK with the salary package you offered (later on, they will give you an increment).

Now is the time. I was waiting for the call from their boss for the 3rd round, which would give my job confirmation, and I wanted to give my best. I did some preparation, learned some topics to be asked in interviews, and finally, I called HR and told them no one was expecting my call, but I didn't stop. HR gave me excuses, I wanted to know the reason for the no response from their side. I called that mam and she

    How to get out of an Unemployment Trap

answered on WhatsApp that my profile was on hold because the boss wanted at least 2 candidates for the job. After that, I didn't receive any response from them. I was being shifted to a relocated location in a week.

This is an example of your selection automatically converting to rejection.

a colleague as an enemy.

Answer the question.

Is your colleague your supportive partner in the office?

In many cases, I found the biggest enemy to be roaming around you in the office. They have the most jealous feelings inside them.

As an example, consider the term "real-world."

During my consultancy job, I used to work on job portals, and my boss gave me the last chance to complete one in 15 days. For help, my colleagues are around me. We didn't have anything in common to make our understanding better. They are doing timepass, and my mistake is that I want to do things on my own. I only had two days before the end of the month to complete my task, and I realized it late.

I have one intern with me from the HR background. So my colleague compares me and her. Secondly, when my boss arrives in the office, they come to me immediately, guide me, and give me instructions to show the boss their helping nature. This is the scenario for some colleagues in the office. Which company should not skip? This is very clear in private small companies to grow their business turnover and make their staff cleaner from the enemy because their working responsibility is the biggest contribution to your success.

Second Example:

I was in contact with one candidate during the first lockdown that arrived in 2020. Women have well-known experience in their fields. They left their jobs for a chance in an environment where they could shift to a new company. After some talk when she trusted me, she told me the actual reason for her living in a pandemic situation, i.e., her office colleagues who didn't treat her well. All time-giving orders and also asked to work continuously.

It's the company proprietors' responsibility to take care of such dedicated employees. And they are not servants, as their colleagues were.

If you have faced such incidents in your life, try to speak up in your interview for a better understanding of the job position and to ensure a good atmosphere.

 How to get out of an Unemployment Trap

Chapter -3
UNEMPLOYMENT ABILITY

If God put you in the human world, then he had planned something for you, so you should live your life with perfection. Instead of complaining. I used to think of myself as an imperfect person who doesn't know how to behave, how to live, and what she wants, but someone said that you always have someone who inspires you to move ahead to achieve your goal. I have that person in the form of "GURU". I always think well when I remember the most motivational sentence, i.e.,

"Strength is Life". Weakness is Death.

So, if choose not to die, you faced the particular situation as do or die situation and came out of it. Because no one is going to take your position, dream, and success for that the Universe sent you to earth. Find it out and the treasure is only yours.

So, my unemployed friends, what did you think about, why you got out of your most suitable job? Is your company not doing well? I guess money is the most crucial problem that Indians have had for so many years.

We don't need to waste time thinking about this. Instead, we have to focus on the next question that I asked you guys to find out. That's why people want to be their own boss.

Let's understand the things before lockdown.

Someone, who appears to be an extrovert, cannot imagine themselves working for someone else and adhering to the company's rules and regulations. So they become entrepreneurs set up the business, invest money and time to become their bosses to work smartly just to gain more profit. And they believe they are highly qualified to be their own CEO.

Now let's move to the things after lockdown.

In India, people are becoming more experienced as they didn't need to depend on anyone else, and this lockdown taught them that things are not permanent as per time and situations, they change into good or bad. So, if you believe you can be hired by someone else, become your own new brand ambassador in both your professional and personal life.

I have seen the scene after the lockdown for 2 years. Most people are begging that someone hire them to work as their advisor so that the job will secure them instead of doing business. But nowadays, people are back to hiring talented candidates and starting to work uniquely in their firms. So you like that as well; why wait for someone to give you an opportunity when you can create your opportunity and spread happiness in your life? You can do all the things. You just have to find your inner talent or hobby that will help you earn money.

Now, a days, parents do allow their children to work flexible hours if they are willing, but not all are fortunate, and they must learn to stand on their own to deal with such problems in life. And for their dreams, they have to become fighters, ambitious, and strugglers to succeed.

How to get out of an Unemployment Trap

Chapter 4
WOMEN'S UNEMPLOYMENT

What should I say about women's unemployment? With her goodwill, they worked hard to secure their position in various corporate sectors. They abandon their studies to marry, and they abandon their jobs to raise a family. Many such employed women take their career decisions in life after lots of challenges and family disbursements, because they understand actual financial values and they have pride in developing a nation.

Women should have to be focused on their goals. They never have to give up their financial independence at any cost.

Financially secure yourself.

Make financial plans for yourself.

I have one of the most dedicated women who is also my cousin's sister in my family. She had chosen her field in computer science, did her MCA, and completed graduation in her hometown, i.e., Burhanpur (MP). She went to Pune city for her job. She continued working even after marriage. She worked at a Delhi company, and she made some tough decisions as well for their children. For a short time, she kept her children at their grandparents' and great-grandparents' homes. Family support made her stronger.

She is my very favourite person in our family. I always admire her and want to become like her. I am pretty sure about it. What I learned from her is that we should always rely on ourselves when making decisions that will help us achieve our goals.

A journey of a girl from a small town, a hard worker, who went outside to change her present life, and she made it happen when the environment of her family is against her decision. But she made her own choices and it's important to make the right choices in life.

Never stop striving for financial independence in your life.

Generation Gap

Why is this generation gap making a move?

When it comes to suspension growth, it's a difference between all generations' levels. Sometimes misunderstandings don't give each other a chance to explain their point of view.

One example

When I went to my private bank for some work, I found a line of 10 people standing in line to go inside. I have contacted a known person inside to take me inside. Before that, when I was standing beside those people, there was a boy who was in row two waiting to go inside. One man directly obtains permission to enter from the person who is being rude to the younger man. That man who is taking a loan will get VIP treatment from the banks. That boy was agitated while standing in line with so many other senior citizens; he was angry at that person, and they were engaged in arguments.

No one was interested at all in listening to the youngest boy's point of view. His point is to treat everyone the same with the same rules and regulations, but no one understands him, and that person just points to that boy, and he intends to prove that boy's mistake only.

The generation gap is not because of age; it's just a number. The actual gap is in your manual confession. Your nature decides how to treat each other.

Judgemental Decision-Making

Many interviewers, clients, and prospective make snap decisions. They didn't understand or see such quality

   How to get out of an Unemployment Trap

candidates' who showed their skills slowly. Like a tortoise, you can win the race slowly.

Self-Growth

When it comes to you, only you have to know what's good or bad for you. Who is loyal to you?

Employees need to develop such quality skills for their better desires to be maintained. If you are in a senior post, you have to be active as compared to your junior staff. Newcomers have taken many courses and skills in their professional experience to get an extra hike into it.

I have seen many students and employees as well who have done courses, generated knowledge in their professions, etc. But I have seen those people who get an opportunity to learn, but then they are uninterested in learning new things.

Update yourself.

You never know who will like us more. Human nature is like their demands; the taste is not constant; it changes every single minute or second. Somewhere, they like your strength and goodness, but they get bored, or you may also get bored knowing that you haven't developed any new qualities, and you may be thinking that you are not able to develop.

Chapter- 5
EMPLOYEES' RISK SEGMENTATION

What is the prospect of students choosing foreign countries for better career growth?

After completing their education, students have to become full-time employees of any firm and start their coding-decoding by working 8–9 hours per day, and after a month, their salary is not enough due to expenses.

Do you underestimate yourself that after leaving this job, you will not find a better job?

Some of my squad people whom I have seen working harder like a machine but not getting a hike in their career. After he fails an interview, he is not confident enough that he will get a direct call from any big company. Nowadays, I have seen Instagram reels. Some people are happy and fine too while working for less salary and enjoying a job as a full-time traveler because they have a flexible job. Apart from the travel companies or MNC companies, some other private sector companies should also start giving a new atmosphere for employees at work because traveling helps understand nature, new religions, places, cultures, and it helps you to gain new ideas in creativity. So creative people should work as they want and get some new ideas for companies' better growth.

So, I suggested that you should join my squad because you live a boring life and are always worried about money and job. I told him not to find any physical therapy or any institute for teaching you better skills to renew your daily working style and to give you the best results, which are not guaranteed.

I told my mother that you are the resources + you are the natural product that developed itself through your natural skills & you are the brand of your product whose goodwill in your performance is equivalent to your better version who attempted his failures examination and passed out within support of self and you will advance in your firm at the same time. People will understand you and learn from your life journey. And sometimes you don't need to wait for anyone to ask about your success stories; instead, you go and share your life journey with them and create goodwill.

I have seen many institutions that have previously opened in India but they only sell online courses for getting a dream job which students try harder to get. Also, I have seen digital media going vast after lockdown, so those institutions have planned and created new varieties just as dishes after making lots of experience in lockdown to cook good food in their home kitchens.

But here is not over, if you are not a good believer who didn't believe in yourself, instead go outside and find those institutions to help you overcome your burdens. This is not a good path for you guys to learn and achieve good results in your lives. After a week of training, those lucky charms will have a better CV filled with good knowledge of degrees, experiences, and many more. So, what is preventing those candidates from flying high in their career journey?

Because of this, some of the people I have seen have started confusing students about making online money. This is the real problem that after the lockdown they are in confusion about backward research in careers as they think that this is the generation that is known for smart work and companies didn't value hard work. But somehow, they have to do with punctuation. Those students are in a dream that with a little hard work and concentration they will earn more money and become their own bosses. That's the actual business growth. Your name or product should be placed online with a reputed website. Then doing business is the easiest thing.

Nowadays, the youngest generation is not getting the importance of both hard work and smart work.

Why are students emigrating to other countries, believing that education and career opportunities are better there, where we can also find good hikes?

After 12th, some students go abroad or go to the most popular colleges in India. Why? to brag about one's degree or to impress in an interview. I have seen the things during Sandeep Maheshwari's motivational videos. Some of them asked about this type of career growth, and Sandeep Maheshwari has explained that no matter where you got your education, the matter is how much knowledge you have gained practically because experience matters most in whatever thing you have learned through hard study to get good marks on the report card.

That's the thing when you have flexible skills, that you are an expert in any career growth. So utilize your skills more than anything else.

But here is not over. Some students like me dream of studying abroad for better understanding, which in India is lower. After our country's independence many years ago, we saw Mahatma Gandhi go to England for better learning and knowledge. Not only he, but many warriors with money and power went outside the country to learn from new cultures, understand things, and return to their country. Some people and students also think that there is a big gap between India's education and education abroad. That is why students who can be flexible with their spending go to such places for higher education. And also, they have very good earnings too, with a particular money hike. And, following the lockdown, which had the greatest impact on education, students were not in the mood to study. They just need some motivation. Why does the school give them space to learn motivation from their favorable master's? One separate lecture on motivation. They can ask for guidance and new ways of making their career so that each will get the direction to achieve something in life

    How to get out of an Unemployment Trap

instead of wasting their time, skills, and knowledge. Because your teachers have a better understanding of you and whether you are an expert in which field. This will help to develop students for the betterment of the country. This lecture is not about moral science; it's about the goal of finding out. And don't be disappointed if your master says no to your career choice; think from both perspectives and try to hear them, their points, and then yours; you don't need to explain it. If after this you still think that you can do it well in your particular field, then go ahead. You will experience that would be good for you. Nothing is wrong, you just have to work hard and be ready to experiment on your own to figure things out.

Why are students emigrating to other countries, believing that education and career opportunities are better there, where we can also find good hikes?

I have my own great example as, for students, ego is the most important thing.

I was taking classes in commerce subject statistics. The scenario was that every commerce student tried at one point to give CA exams and I was also one of them. One day in my last second year of graduation from BCom, I and my friend went to our tuition teacher to ask for coaching for the entrance exam of CA. He said that come at a different time and along with your parents. We didn't understand his answers. My friend went in the afternoon, and I went with my father in the evening. He asked me about my percentage and why I wanted to be a CA. And in a few seconds, my mind was blown down, and broke my heart when he said, "Don't waste time and money on it for which you are not good enough." For that, you need stamina, energy to learn things, and a lot more. My father also explained that thing and we went home, but here I am not OK with the decision and I have decided to experience it on my own. I took two exams by asking for money from my dad's friend and also from my brother-in-law. I have planned things with low investment and more effort as I didn't have money but had a lot of courage. I took study material from my school friend who passed the entrance exam and one who was with me to ask our statistics sir to teach us, so I have arranged study material. Now I have to clear some concepts. I am very stable in explaining what the inline lecturer taught me in the lecture.

I have taken a one-year free study plan from an online institution that just started at that time, and they have given one year to CA CPT students to encourage most of the students to connect with them online. And since then, I've made an effort to learn new things, planned my entire day's schedule, and studied in a room that is hot during the summer. Aside from that, I received assistance from my brother, Jogesh Jain, who arranged for his friend Bala, the most experienced accountant, to teach me online about reconciliation statements, and I have lower results because I did well and made a good effort in finding study materials on my own, arranging money, and utilizing things so well that I can't tell what I learned from this experiment. Sometimes it's just not enough to win arguments or aid, sometimes you have to think about what is good for you.

If you failed without making an effort, that's different, and if you failed after a lot of effort, that's different.

And also, if you talk to people with any effort, it's useless, but if you listen to them after your efforts and find out the reason why you are not succeeding, that's different.

So why do I decide to find out the reason on my own instead of blindly believing in the master's decision? Sometimes you have to find out on your own.

Communication

Sometimes communication mismatches with your seniors, as you try harder to create a career and a family, but the most important thing is to mould yourself in a way that you can

                How to get out of an Unemployment Trap

handle multiple things together.

I've seen many women, even from my school squad, handle the household, get involved in business, and live like a housewife. And some were looking forward to getting married to a job person. These people work hard to feed their children.

So, I just want to say that as girls they have to make some practical decisions instead of emotional ones, and that's the real growth of their dreams to achieve in life.

I have not achieved anything in my life and have never overcome my failure, but then again, I am not over because I still have that much courage to try hard till I achieve something, and this book is not for helping you to achieve success or any goal, but it is all about hope. Until and unless your hope is alive, you are alive to take action, otherwise, you will always be called the weakest person in the world.

Just imagine how hard you worked to achieve success. Everyone has an untold story and each of them is a real hero as they work hard and willing to take risks in their career and life. They are the biggest achievers in their life, so think about it. When no one is there to help you understand what you believe in, you stand up for yourself to achieve it.

I have written one affirmation in my mobile notes but I never open it and read it because I am sometimes willing to see new ways of motivation from the universe, sometimes from particular people who motivate as well as demotivate me, but I must have the grace to see myself achieving a big goal in life. Because the powerful dream dissolved toxic people's thinking after our dream come true. Till then, let them help you in both ways to rise in the world and take action. And powerful people never give up hope or abandon their dreams. And believe in the universe's energy, then find the way and begin walking on that path.

For dreamers, I only say this: if you ever fail in life and think that your growth will be best at a particular age or you can achieve the goal, then before taking the action to change your current situation, just say the reason why.

1. After taking step 1, let's just try harder as you've got a second chance to achieve your dream.

What will be the result? By achieving your goal, you will become a hero.

Let's take an example: if a scientist fails in 100 attempts and then works on their theory and experience, he will almost certainly try the 101 attempt's again with the mindset of "let's do it again even if it fails, but what if it succeeds."

2. If a scientist before becoming a scientist starts thinking that if I do not become a scientist, then what? And what if I become a scientist? The things which will come from his end will not be major in terms of success, but he will help a lot of people in life. Then never think about it again. Just stay focused.

Women's Unemployability

Let me share with you an untold short story about my friend in the corporate sector. Here is the start at a private company, in which 15 trainees are learning the work of a travel company. My friend's role is to book trips and dissolve quarries with a good solution. But she was a trainee, so her main focus was to learn the things which their TL taught them in 3 months. After 3 months, when she got a good position, which meant she got an important working department, instead of learning, she left the job.

Why? During the training period, she went to the office, where she made new friends. They were also learning and growing, like our senior department, who came to meet us on the very first day to guide us to increase interaction, etc. While they were in the training room, they entertained us by singing songs, cracking jokes, and sharing amusing stories, as well as guiding us on how to behave in corporate settings. Things

			How to get out of an Unemployment Trap

were going well for her because she was innocent girl who was non-talkative. She instead interacted with some friends slowly and each had an affair outside or in the office. Only she was a single girl, and one of his college Maharashtrians also had no girlfriend because he was not matured. Everyone in the training room cracked jokes about him, and he also couldn't do things well.

He knew it and that's why he made some of the situations like he made him think about that girl as his GF, he taught everything to that boy, he told some lies about it, and due to a little interaction, he felt something different in his own mind. He thought that the girl also liked him, but he couldn't say as they wanted boys to speak first on this topic. So, during the training, there was very little time to complete training, so our TL decided let's play something. So during the game, that boy got the chance and his colleague made things easy for him. He was so successful in his mind games that he convinced his foulest friend about that girl. That day, he asked that girl to propose to her. As per game rules, the person has to pick one dare or one truth, and that fool picked the dare as he was already an entertainer for everyone in the training room. That day, everyone made a joke about the girl using that boy's name, and everyone had created their own story in their mind. After this, it was also not over here as in the office, that girl cleared that she didn't think similarly about him and she just interacted as a friend. That boy, after rejection, told everyone lies, and to make her happy, he lied to those with whom she stayed in the office, those were her friends. And after that, the girl told him to complain or leave the job, to which TL replied, "Let the things dissolve; I will not let him do anything about you; your department after on boarding will be different, so concentrate on your work."

That girl started things doing well after ignoring everything, but after that, some of her colleagues acted like enemies to her and started making jokes about her again in the office, and the girl left her job.

I asked her to complain, but she told me that nothing happened wrong, it was just mental harassment, and I don't want to increase it. So leave it. I am a middle-class girl and I got a chance to live life alone in a big city, so I don't want to miss it. Every girl's parents grew their daughters with the vision that one day they would make them proud. Culture and society already interfere with their freedom, but my father gave me that freedom, so I have to take care of it and focus on how to make them proud of me. That was my last goal before getting married, she said

This is also an example of women's unemployability as some of the women are still fighting for freedom which they didn't get from the world, and that's the reason why they have to take the hardest decisions for themselves to stop any mental stress. For them, self-response is a bigger thing than anything else in life. Why do they have to take one step down instead of making that creep outside?

Girls have to become independent women.

Girls need to become independent women.

Girls, you have to become an independent women before getting married. No matter if you get your parents', boyfriend's, or friends' support or not it doesn't matter. What matters is when you learn the things which are right for you at that particular moment, you don't need anyone's support behind this. Just take your right path and start walking on it without hoping or expecting anyone's helping hands to guide you. One day, they will understand why you have chosen this path.

Girls are the ones who are born to create something new. You make their family think of things differently. Girls make new life optimizations to which their families say yes; the girl has a new way of looking at culture, which will help our new generation of kids to follow and improve it rather than pointing

     How to get out of an Unemployment Trap

out any inconvenience to follow only the oldest rituals.

Girls, you only need to wake up; your other challenging people will, later on, wake up. And it's not about girls only. Some boys are also helping nature, they help their children with the same efforts. It's all about balancing your problems, goals, happiness, and achievement in life.

Let's start with a brilliant love story between two people—

I always watch Instagram reels before sleeping, and one day I was watching Instagram reels, which blew my mind and made me wish for falling stars from the darkest sky. I have seen only the youngest couple. They were around on job and had completed a few years in corporate sectors in the same country. They were both college friends. Maybe I didn't remember. The boy is in IT engineering and has been working in India for a long time, whereas the girl got the opportunity to work in India before moving abroad. The interesting part of the story is that they both never told each other they liked each other, as they were always together and never thought that someone had to move, so they never spoke to each other. The boy knew well that the girl was very ambitious and he didn't want to stop her from flying high.

So when the girl told his friend about going abroad, they also discussed that they couldn't live without each other. It's the biggest problem to handle and decide, whether it's in favor of professional life or whether it's personal due to which girls have to give up on their ambitions for that person. But the twist was the IT boy had given up on his job and decided to move abroad with his love, and in 3 weeks' they got married and moved abroad.

Things are not completed yet as the boy sometimes cooks food for both of them. They discuss expenses, they discuss money, they discuss their happiness, and making their lives balanced as they both want everything things together. That's the real meaning of togetherness.

So, as a mediator, we know we've never had that person in our lives, and we've never had that support from our family either. So at that time, you need to become an independent woman without wasting time waiting for someone who will never come to you. As you know, such things are not possible, but the possibility rises in you that you need to stand over yourself to support yourself.

I am telling you these things, which sound harsh too, but they are important because some girls are dreamers, they never stop dreaming day or night, and some ambitious girls, due to low financial power, need to give up on their dream. Those who dream of moving to foreign countries do so not only for the sake of freedom but also because it allows them to think of new things and try new things.

I have seen some girls have a lot of courage to make their career a way that they should move to a higher place and achieve something better because that higher place gives them free space, but those girls can't get it as most of the love stories happen with some possibility and some which are impossible, so for that reason, girls who don't need to be dependent, just need to stand over themselves and make the best of it. That's why I wrote, "Girls need to become independent women."

Don't wait for the right time, the right reason, or the right person. Instead, become your own right person.

Education impacted girl's life and their cultural life which I was a little bit bothered.

I have two different ways to explain about it

1st I have seen in my circle in the girl's group that the topper is now a housewife by their own choice or by family or her own and her husband's side too. Due to those cultural things, the girls make it easy for them to point to each girl, as they may be not able to tell their family what is good for them.

    How to get out of an Unemployment Trap

Find your uniqueness.

Your unique ability

Why are you on Earth as a human being? You could be an animal or a non-living thing, but why are you here and what is your problem telling you? Why did God choose you for such a painful life? Discover its connectivity. Everything connected reflects only on you. Find it out.

In a notebook or mobile notes, write all your good things, your likes, hobbies, dreams, and everything, and on the other hand, write bad things about you which are affecting you. I have written these things and thought about whether they help me to make money in which I was interested. I found the things which I like as a hobby. I have the talent and potential to make them my assets in life. I just need to make them more expressive to show them off publicly and then to the world.

If you were trying something new, share it with those who doubt you; then you have people who are always willing to help you, and sometimes they never tell you negative things about your efforts, which will hurt you.

Don't lose your hopes when you will not get the expected results. Just try out things and make them perfect and then see the result, but remember how much you do work on it. That much you will get the result.

And one more important thing is that in each step you take, just trust in your judgment instead of those people who always underestimate you. Sometimes they were right because at that time you were making efforts to make it perfect and they only helped you to be perfect by demotivating you. After you got hurt, the extra work turned into success. And don't try to make your imagination work because many people know that a dreamer ruins their moment by picturing things in advance and not putting forth any effort. Success can come to you in any kind of way if you want it to. If someone wants to come into your life, then they will find a way to come to you. That means you don't need to do anything as things happen naturally, and that's why I like nature.

A very difficult task for every woman and man is to make their parents feel proud of them.

Is it right? Is it a very difficult task for you guys to make your parents proud?

If yes, then don't you try it? Because you will try harder and waste a few years of your life making your parents proud. Instead, focus on your dreams. Become ambitious, confident, self-believing, and make your path right. If you feel proud of what you did and achieved, then one day your parents will also feel it.

In a woman's life, their father's importance is much more important than anything else. Those girls will never make their dad's name down in any way. Instead, they will work hard to make their name visible more and by her name, her father's name will also be visible.

One example: one day, during a conversation with my sister, we were discussing how important it is for a girl to marry soon. I have been thinking about it in my mind. Is marriage causing girls to stay away from freedom and peace? For men, it's just like they have to give up their bachelor life, but for girls, she has to go away from their place, family, and everything. So that's a big question for girls to get married. Isn't it implied that boys should have to leave their parent's home to be independent with their new family? It's not only for not taking responsibility, but it's also a good idea that boys should have to travel from their original location to the newer location; why should rituals be reserved for girls only?

But, in our conversations, she told us that as a 'girl' we just do something for our dad and that is to get married. Apart from this, nothing is there to feed our father and make us their lovely daughter. Frankly speaking, I am not satisfied with this answer. I know some of my readers were also not satisfied with

          How to get out of an Unemployment Trap

this answer.

It looks like a very difficult task because our parents' wishes are different from ours and also simple, but we don't want what our parents find for us. Just remember one thing my readers, our parents create a way for us to simply and easily get things, but we are a most confused generation who make it difficult. We were perplexed when it comes to selecting a life partner, a career, and our comfort. But our parents will work until the day they die to provide us with something that will fulfill our wishes and make us happy for the rest of our life. But we did get their path of what they were doing for us.

Our fathers live with their daughters in a very strict environment. Sometimes they live with their sons just because they know very well that men have to be stronger than anyone else and never expect anyone else's emotional support till that time. They must have been super strong in life.

Second, the most important thing in a woman's life is that she has to become unemployed for her family, including her husband and kids. And if they get the chance to be employed, then they also have to make management of both professional responsibilities as well as family responsibilities by themselves. They never expect unconditional support because they understand it is all about her wishes instead of all. They know that it is not a woman's duty to make meals for her husband all the time. They know that it is not only her wife's need to fulfill all the wishes of her kids. As they both got married, responsibility was equally divided. No matter in their relationship, which duty their wife chose, they make life easy because in their relationship, gender is not important to decide such responsibility.

Chapter-6
BUSINESS DEVELOPMENT PLANS

Every business has its development plans. But I have three important people who are the most affordable ways to become a businessman and earn money in millions of dollars.

1 Self-Employed

2 Entrepreneur

3 Business Men with Investors and Employees

1 Self-Employees

Let me tell you guys that I know my readers are more intelligent in understanding this. But I want to make it more understandable based on unemployable ones. As we can see, COVID-19 has affected many people's lives and it's also not a business's mistake that they have done anything wrong because everyone has the right to do something, to achieve something.

If I was not wrong, many of the younger generation people, like those from 18 to 30, have a business mindset, and also some employees, like those from 35 to above, have a lot of experience and hard workers in that firm have the thought of doing business and those employees were thought to quit the job before lockdown with whatever money and knowledge they have achieved. And these people will do things like use their skills, knowledge, and mastermind in production to launch it. They will be able to do it because they have the money to invest in their product, marking, and selling. They can become self-employed. Self-Employed didn't require anyone's help in launching products and making a profit because, in this category, people do things on their own.

And if they were fired from the company, then they didn't need to worry at all, as they had their platform where they could walk on their own with baby steps. I want to tell them that whatever plans they were making, kindly do it if they were talented because they did not need to find the workers, as there were most of the people who wanted to do something looking for an opportunity. But self-employed people didn't like to increase the scale of their company and wanted to earn money in a higher range. That's why they learned skills to use and by themselves alone they want to earn money. That's why they are self-employed.

2 Entrepreneurs: If you think that entrepreneurs help businesses in doing their biggest deals with risky decisions, then why didn't they help themselves to make such business deals to earn a whole profit?

But things changed after the lockdown, as businessmen changed the way of making money, as they previously used. After the lockdown, many businesses and companies found that they were only making money offline and that there was no use of digital marketing. But after the lockdown, businessmen found such things and started asking for new techniques, and due to that, it affected those kinds of employees who were not smart and had no knowledge of it, and due to that, they got fired. There were many more reasons, but I am using this reason to make an understanding for all readers.

So I have plans for entrepreneurs to make decisions that are affordable for them and their businesses. But it's quite not good for such employees, due to which they lose their job. In such a case, the company fired those candidates who were not productive and did not perform well in their jobs. And also, after the lockdown, companies are focusing on their company growth instead of their company's scale.

But if someone can take risks, that person should never panic in any kind of situation. Instead, that person will focus on a solution. So, they will need to invest money and time in learning skills.

But, after developing their company, they must call on

those loyal candidates and give them work who also cares for the company.

Entrepreneurs with an investor and employees-During lockdown, businessmen and employees have faced so many things for which businessmen need to take the hardest decision. Businesses' strategy is to reduce expenses and overcome spending on such things. Because of that, they can be able to save some money. So they decided to fire some employees and use the remaining money to continue making utensils as well as technology. Because reducing the scale of employees will be better than anything else. It's an important decision for them to get back on their path of earning money, for which customers have made it less important to buy such products. But this decision has affected many of those candidates who were dependent on the particular job and never had the mindset that one day their company would fire them. And in this category, those employees have the mindset of doing business, not having any other source of making money. They were begging people via LinkedIn to get good anywhere, from any source of money, because they needed it. Previously, candidates did share their expectations of doing work in the following things: preferable location, salary, and many things as per their experience and knowledge. However, they did not have a choice at the time. They just need a job and some money per month.

So, any people who were making business plans should have to go ahead with confidence to create a new brand in the market with their own money and with jobless people so that the percentage of unemployees will also be reduced. I advised that if you have the knowledge and skills, then no one will stop you from making such an innovative thing.

Before Lockdown and After Lockdown: Before Lockdown, the competition of passing Interviewers was already high and they had several reasons to judge you after walking to

          How to get out of an Unemployment Trap

the interviewer's door, sitting on the chair in front of them, and leaving that place. They always have top status, which a simple candidate never reaches. And, following Lockdown, their confidence in judging such candidates in such matters increased. And unfortunately, unemployed people need to face the toughest question of why they got fired from the particular job where they have given their whole life working for the same company. And if they weren't satisfied, then their minds were fulfilled by the toxic thought that the company had fired him. Then he might have had a bad reason or status in the previous company, or maybe he had no productive mindset to work.

Many of us understand the emotions of such people in India, but we think that we should take some practical decisions. But it is not an equivalent decision.

Some companies come ahead to give the job to the unemployed ones, but they are making use of their poor condition by giving jobs at a lower salary to which that job was vacant for so many long times. Is it OK? And the problem is if we think according to that unemployed person, he never asks them as they need it.

Answer the Question: How will you ask them for a salary hike?

Before the lockdown, I'm sure the employees had asked for a salary hike while maintaining their work, holidays, and punctuation. But after the lockdown, if we see an unemployed person who has recently joined, he will not ask his boss to increase his salary.

But what about the candidate who has just got their first job? They also try such things to work hard till the probation period ends, and after impressing, they must go for an increased salary. It's a rule that after six months, the company himself increases the salary. In such a company, within three months, they increase the salary based on employees' hard work.

Is there a company that will pay you even if you are not

doing your work properly?

Tax consultant Firm: It's been 40 days since the hardest time and energy were given to the tax consultant company. The person was doing billing work from 10 a.m. to 7 p.m., i.e., entering bills into the bookkeeping account, and she was doing it in one day at a high speed. She usually completes four of five files per day with other work given to her by the Receptionist. Apart from billing work, she was not confident about doing balance sheets on her own and she used to confirm each thing with her helpers, who were not much help in the office. But she used to work and learn new things and utilize them in her work.

But things went wrong as the environment of that place was not healthy and they ignored the determination of that girl. Now the one month is over and the girl was doing billing jobs apart from the balance sheet making of that particular file. She accepted that she was not perfect in this work, but what about the time she gave to that firm for one month and some more days in addition? The firm has not paid her one month's salary and they lied to her that they would give it when they debit salary to staff members. She waited more than 40 days for the salary and worked there, but the person was ignoring her and also the staff member who got the salary.

Is it good that the time you invest in such a company and also work there with a little bit of productivity? But in the end, they didn't pay you for such work. Clint has paid the company for which the girl has worked. But they have not thought to give payment of one month to that girl who has tallied all the bills in her book of accounts.

This was a real example of how to understand the nature of employees and companies. Aside from the fact that 99 percent of the time you are not working, the company must compensate you for devoting your time to completing such work.

          How to get out of an Unemployment Trap

Timing of our success.

Our success came at the right time.

What is the exact time to succeed in a specific goal in which we have worked so hard for so many years, falling repeatedly, but only one feeling and thought made us achieve that, to stand up to get it? How badly do you want that thing in your life?

But some negative stuff ruins your success. Your actual success is when you stop thinking about society, culture, and the people around you. When you are right, just be right on your path. Later on, your success will convince them that you were right. Don't waste energy on surpassing their ideas; convince them.

When you stop thinking about each of them, then your actual success will arrive in your life. Simply concentrate on what you have planned to create.

Progress reports

Actual knowledge

Every employee needs these three things for earning; a hike in salary; and a better career opportunity. Unfortunately, you were young, so what will you be doing? I am going to ask such people that whatever experience they got on their CV is directly updated from God, yes really from God or such candidate's hard work made that experience. If my readers' second answer will be theirs, then let me tell you about one incident of a young candidate.

The boss required around 10 years of experience from the youngest candidate, whose age was around 23–24 years old. That candidate asks them to at least give me the chance to show you how much potential I have at work and how much I care for the company as a loyal candidate.

What makes you feel like switching your job?

Corporate atmosphere

Working conditions are not good.

Demotivating

Is it worth it to give a chance to a fresh candidate? If any of the companies are not giving you a chance to gain experience, then how will they get an experienced candidate? But some companies are worried about the fact that after developing new skills with that firm, their employees will switch to that particular company to move to a higher place with higher hikes in salary.

What makes people move from their particular country to another country?

For more opportunities

For experiencing new places,

For additional salary increases

As we can see, many employees from India go to Australia, Canada, Russia, Dubai, and other places.

1 For more opportunities: People chose the country and city where they would have the most opportunities to work in their dream job. Apart from getting married, many women like to move to foreign countries because they want to live independently. And, after the lockdown, I've noticed that many people have improved their skills and used their time to learn new things; they are very happy doing work at flexible times as a freelancer, and they have no desire to do a dream job; instead, they choose jobs that pay them more. Lockdown has brought many changes in human beings, as they are not willing to work according to their own time and skills. And it's very important that if you have such skills and knowledge, then no one will bother you for doing that particular job. And nowadays, people have created such a mindset that they should work on their own instead of doing that particular job that was more time-consuming and also didn't get that much money.

2 For experiencing - These are some of the people who are

     How to get out of an Unemployment Trap

eager to learn new things outside of culture. It means they are very creative and like to develop new things and create new ways for people, and they first think big, which will help the people, and then they will make their own money out of it.

And if I can say that those employees moved to a new city for a new era in their lives, They want to make a good family who never think about culture or society when they go ahead with their development.

3. For salary hikes—those employees like to go abroad to grab career opportunities. A career path is a lifeline thing since anyone can do anything from anywhere. They want to reach a higher place in their career but they didn't get a good return in the amount of money in India or their particular place. So that's why they want to go abroad and want to earn more money before their retirement.

Chapter-7
EDUCATION-BASED CAREER OPPORTUNITIES

If you want to become a pilot, then the 10th is much more important for you. If you want to become a CA, then the 12th is much more important for you. But if you want to become a scientist, then experiments are much more important than making good marks on the results of boards. However, you took these above courses for study, but you will get perfect after practicing harder and doing experiments for a better experience. Until then, you will not become perfect at flying till you learn the equipment of the plane and practice hard to fly high. You will not become a perfect CA until you start working professionally at a particular firm. There will be no use of authority because simply studying and acquiring theoretical knowledge is insufficient to become practically perfect. And until you use that particular theory in an experiment to become a scientist, no one will help you better than you alone.

Similarly, students must gain practical knowledge in their specific fields at a young age to face challenges because, to achieve their dream, goal, and success, students must face challenges.

We have all seen the success stories of such players who won gold medals for India, as they already know that their perfection must be in the game rather than anything else. If they lose energy, they will fail. But what about educated related stories in which you will also fail if you do not study? If you do not understand such a topic, then you will not learn it by working hard. Your teacher will prepare you to crack that particular exam, but you will not pass until you work hard enough.

After 12th completion, most of the students go to the

most highly educated colleges to study a particular course. This shows that you have taken a degree from a higher college, which helps you with placement too. But is it beneficial that the job which you got from the particular and you have not completed their targets? Then they will fire you for the reason that you have not worked properly. What will the college do? They only promised you to grab opportunities and placement, but you have to do it on your own in the rest of the things. It's just that theoretical knowledge helps you pass exams, but practical knowledge helps you stay alive in that particular job after placement. So try to understand the importance of money. If you learn how to earn money, then there will be no use for particular degrees, experience, or anything else.

I have seen that many students get confused and don't use their brains and think that after doing this course it will be better to work in that job and they take different courses from online sites to develop their skills in it. However, you must consider it in the context of earning money. Some people developed skills to improve their CVs and get interviews, and once they get that job, they will be paid. But if you want to earn money as a freelancer or business, then it will be most important for you to earn money on your own socially.

Before Lockdown, people had the choice of being self-employed for self-freedom, which means they wanted their own time to work and earn money. However, after the lockdown, they discovered that in working sectors, your skills will help you survive longer and earn money instead of that job, which has no security because they can fire you at any time and from anywhere.

If a company tells you to sign a bond with them for 2 years or more than 2 years, then why don't you have the right to sign a bond with them that the company will not fire you till that particular year? Because, following the lockdown, we have all seen the majority of the 30-40 year employees lose their jobs after years of loyal service. And now they are begging for jobs in the necessary areas.

What if a second lockdown arrives?

We are all certain that self-employed people will be more addicted to working in the second lockdown, including me and my readers. Apart from them, employees who were doing work under one of the superbly knowledgeable companies. They will be more focused and not worry if they lose their job because they know how to work on their skills and maintain themselves well in the corporate sector. And in those potential employees' mindsets, one thing will rise: how to become the best seller of a particular product while sitting at home and taking health precautions to see it.

Yes, after the first lockdown, some people, including businesses, discovered that having a physical store for their product is critical. So they will digitally increase their business. But they will still face the problem of selling their product socially. It's a different thing that you have developed your business and opened new stores as well as expanded your business in a wide range of cities. But after ordering the product, the person will face the problem of delivering goods to a particular customer in the lockdown, as the same thing happened in the first lockdown.

So, the better is that they should go through their nearest store and buy the products and utensils, and for that, the particular stores should need to develop their websites and product information sharing in a wider range. If they were already famous stores in the particular area, then there would be no need to do much marketing.

We have all seen that many people have changed their products within a day or night and most of them have started selling things like vegetables, foods, and breakfast items as per the necessity of their customers, as we have learned in supply

          How to get out of an Unemployment Trap

and demand of products. The golden rule of economics is that demand will increase, then selling will also increase, and if demand changes, then buyers of a product will also be changed. So people have started selling such products according to the necessity of the customers to earn money.

In a lockdown, a man whom customers give money for their order for that product, that person is selling cookies and other things in the colony to whom customers will eat their breakfast.

The food business was merely affected by COVID-19 as we all have seen one video going viral on FB in a foreign country, maybe in the US. The man had a large number of potatoes to sell to the customers and their turnover was much better before the lockdown. But after facing one year of lockdown without doing business and earning money, they faced new things, i.e., they needed to sell those potatoes and also faced a lot of loss from not making any sales of their potatoes. And after that, they shared the particular video only to get people's attention and make them aware of such things that people were not selling fresh food, instead, they were selling foods that were not sold in lockdown.

So, it's a big question to think that what product will not be affected by such things as COVID-Crisis and that will work in Lockdown too. Digital sector people were happy that they would make money in lockdown too and also in medicine stores and hospitals.

I will provide you with the idea, but you have to find the solution for the nation.

But what about the unemployed who were not working during the first lockdown and are still looking for work during the second?

The corporate sector has made the mistake of firing those candidates who needed money during the lockdown. And after that, for those who were facing problems getting through the first round of interviews, the strictness was increased in the professional sectors due to which they were still making efforts to clear the rounds of interviews. I think the simplicity of the person helps to understand his character and his passion for work is enough to know that he is a dedicated servant of the company. So I just want people to provide jobs for the jobless. Because in India, talented people are larger, but we disrespect the talent and those people who go outside the country and help their country in developing sectors.

country's future growth and its loss.

After the lockdown, two things got damaged in India at a higher rate, i.e., unemployed people increased, and also some valuable loss in the education system. The newly graduated candidate who graduated under lockdown has faced the problem of getting a job easily in such a firm. But it is a different thing. But due to the lockdown, some of the students forget the importance of education and this has ruined the future of the country.

But if uniqueness comes in the education sector and also in the minds of corporate people, then it will be helpful for the future growth of the country. Those who face rejection are the ones who will bring that kind of innovation to the future generation. Because those who understand the value of rejection will not allow their newcomer to face the same issue again in the future.

   How to get out of an Unemployment Trap

Chapter- 8
SELF DEVELOPMENT

If you want to bring change to something, in people or a country, then first bring the change to yourself, and after that, the changes will take you up in your own life.

I know most of the starting difficulties people face when they are mentally stressed and, due to that, anxiety, depression, and panic attacks take place. And those people who are under this category deal with the daily problems in life regarding family, job, and money. And the corporate sector makes use of them by putting them under job stress, and those who are insecure about their jobs work harder even if their work is perfect.

Talk to Yourself

When no one understands you, you must stand up for yourself and help yourself.

I still remember the day when I felt depressed and tried hard to speak a word to myself, but yes, it has given me relief, and later on, I realized that talking to yourself doesn't mean that you were mentally disturbed or had a mental disorder. Instead, it helps you fight such mental problems. I always talk to myself and share things that I want. After that, I automatically work on the solution that helps me come out of that problem. We can support ourselves, which is beneficial to trust instead of judging. It prefers to help to make you more secure so that no one will get to know about your problems till you can share them. So it is better to become stronger by helping yourself. Yes, sometimes you need someone to listen to your words, hug you, and spread love and happiness with you. But when you started helping yourself, then you didn't need anything from anyone.

Share your disability.

First of all, you failed in front of people in achieving those particular things as they didn't take you on a serious note and also didn't help you out of it. And the second time you failed in front of yourself when you didn't believe in yourself. So, if you want to be successful in life, try to make this both positive and, as a result, no one can stop you, even if you try to stop yourself. But your heartbeats take you to that path where you want to go.

So, the main point here is to understand that you should try to overcome all your fears and stand in front of those who didn't think it was good for you to get an achievement in it. Share your flaws with them, admit that you are not perfect, and conceal your efforts to surprise them with your success.

Why did our family, friends, and teachers not take us seriously?

Its answer is only in one sentence, that we did hide our seriousness from them while we were at home, with friends, or in front of our teachers, and for that reason, they didn't take us very seriously.

If we talk about family atmosphere, then things are from our childhood. We have given rights to our relatives and family members to tell us anything, and we dismiss the war by saying that it's a bond with your cousins and family members and they tell you in a joking way. But is it a joke or you are the Joker of your family that anytime anywhere they can tell you anything, insult you and also disrespect you? So, try to create a respectful environment with your kids and not let them be insulted by any of their relatives, even if they are your most important people in life.

Similarly, we tried things harder to share our private lives with our friends, and sometimes we get to know that your importance in their lives is not much, as they have most of the important friendship groups of two or three members. But the thing is, the bond with your friends is different from your family members, and that's the big thing.

But it looks a little different when you share your ability and dream with the particular teacher whom you treat as a favorite teacher or guardian, and after they tell you that it is not a goal for you by judging your personality with that goal, it leaves you a little bit disappointed.

Control your temper and don't be addicted to anything.

I do have one word to say that people are addicted to overthinking, which creates some disabilities in your goal and also means you missed the opportunity at a particular time. Because after giving 100 percent and after investing most of the years in preparation for that achievement, you want, and at present, if you didn't work harder and give your best, then it affected your results and you need to face failure. Because no one will be able to see your efforts, they only want results. And the main point is that you just need to control such things in life and not be addicted to anything that affects your success.

concentration.

Concentrate on your own words, what you said, what you know, and what you understood, to become aware of any misunderstanding. Being a dreamer, I am lax in making efforts to achieve that dream in real life. And to overcome that laziness, I should have a solid reason for doing such things in my life. Concentration comes from the seriousness you show towards that thing. Due to this, your mind will be stable and who has told you to wake up at 5:00 am to get success or work late at night to get success? Those who succeed have found their comfort zone, a place to work peacefully, and a place to study peacefully. But my dear reader, try to find your own peaceful time when you are comfortable doing something for success. Every person is unique, whether their surface of work or study subject is the same, but you are unique and your success will also be different, so it's important to find your way of achieving that particular dream.

Self-Believe

I do like people who live their lives as per their preferences. They do not ask anyone for what they want, which will be the choices and whatever they do, it's just because they have self-belief and also have the capability to handle risk in life.

Instead of complaining about your problems, continue your work to achieve that goal.

Be aware of mind gamers, which disturb your mind, your life, and most things. If you are right, don't waste time proving that you are right in those particular things.

Take a risk.

Through your frustration somewhere.

 How to get out of an Unemployment Trap

Chapter-9
Positive Affirmation

Positive Affirmation comes out by keeping a positive attitude, even if you haven't achieved anything, because that's the difference between you and others. Try to give your full support to yourself. If you help yourself, then only you will be able to help others. Trust yourself, appreciate your efforts, which directly connect you with motivation, and always think good for yourself, as Swami Vivekanand Ji has written.

You become exactly what you think.

Try to get some positive affirmations online or do yoga, or you can also listen to positive voices from motivational applications, but it's really important to build your mind and open your own heart. So I have created a few lines of affirmation for myself, which I didn't do daily, but yes, when it was necessary, I did it continuously for some time.

Note: You can write it in any language, and I have written it in Hindi.

I can do anything. Whatever happened, let it go. I can do anything I want. Nothing is left for me to do. I love myself, and I can trust myself. I will always be happy with myself. I want to see a smile on my face. I want to thank God that whatever you wanted to make me realize, I understood it, and from now on I will make sure to take care of my dream and succeed in life.

-Think well of yourself: - By doing this, some good messages reflect on your ears, mind, and heart, due to which you will get positive energy and you will like to do each task even if it was a boring day or boring life. You can make your points based on your ability, like if you were the most negative person like me, then try to create some points based on it to get rid of it.

1. I am the best.

2. I am the most intelligent and cool person.

3. People are drawn to my ideas.

4. I can do anything that I want.

5. I love my family.

6. I can do anything perfectly in a short amount of time.

7. I can sense the presence of God.

8. I love myself.

9. One day I will achieve my dream in real life.

10. I am unique.

Stay Away from such negativity: -this is the most important point for my readers to understand and find out. Those people, places, and things that affect your positivity should get away from them. They might not stop till your death, so you just need to get away from them and find the surface where you like the most. And don't try to answer them rudely; instead, let your success silence their mouth. Sometimes, if you have not made any preparations, anything that is good for you to achieve a particular thing, then only hope can work, and due to that hope, which is alive in your mind and heart, can never make you down, never try to live your path, and also never throw you out of the dreamy life.

In my struggling life, I got rejections, I got failures, I got negativity, people judged me, and also no one trusted me except me, so I always and always appreciated my hard work. Just like I was a student and I got good comments from my favorite teacher, that's become for me the biggest appreciation note that I can do something due to which people will not praise me, instead, I feel good.

Celebrate Failure

In my life, job seeking was the biggest failure for me, and that's the reason I have struggled for a long time to learn, understand and take knowledge about corporate sectors to

 How to get out of an Unemployment Trap

write this book. I am sure that things will not end over here, but if we together make effort, then it will be the easiest thing to achieve something and make our country proud. My only motive behind writing this book is to overcome the percentage of unemployed people and those rejected candidates. They shouldn't need to constantly look for jobs that will give them money. Instead, they will find their path and source to get money, and they will be the strongest people who earn money independently.

But how will you celebrate the things you have without money? Then try the things you like the most; watching movies, watching matches, making something with your talents; that's the great thing. For example, if I don't have any money in my pocket and I want to express such thoughts, I write a poem that will become a memory of that particular situation-based thought, as I have written a poem in my struggling life that Khwabo hi Khwabo meh. Or if I have some money, at least 10 rs to eat Pani Puri and make my mood good. I still remember the day when I was having my birthday and I had no money in my hand. I did not get any monetary help from my caring and helping nature parents to feel the good vibes. I tried out things to check my pockets, bags, and other things and from there I found some coins and notes of 10-20 RPs. I bought the things which will be more memorable for me for a long time. So try to appreciate your life journey because you were the only hero in it and you will get help to share it in your untold story.

Learn from Mistakes

Make Use of Your Mistakes: One of the first mistakes we make is blindly trusting anyone, even if they are our favourites, family members, friends, or anyone else. And when we do such things as a favour, they don't expect anything from you, as they didn't do anything in return for you. They instead ask you a silly question: why did you do this for me? I never asked you to do this for me.

So, try to keep your emotions aside and concentrate on your own goal to be achieved by yourself without anyone else's help.

One thing I have observed is that such people are afraid of doing something in a new way. They don't know how to make a fresh start, and they are always afraid of not doing anything and also sad that they didn't get success in it.

I want to tell them that don't keep any restrictions on themselves, as from childhood till your death, their parents, life partner, teachers, and children keep those restrictions for them, and for that reason, they get afraid of doing something new or you get scared of choosing that path on which no one will help you out. Such things you have to do on your own. And that's the biggest mistake of your life. Sometimes, you go to your friends for some freshness. They will never judge you, will never stop you from what you want to do, and who will always be with you, trusting you even if you are wrong. They want to see you happy, so that's why they didn't stop you.

I will give an example: -In my childhood, I used to hide my talent to share it with anyone, as I am a shy girl. I sketched a boy sitting alone on a stone, and also painted the whole drawing while I was doing the final work on it. But my friend picked it up and took it to our class teacher's hand, and she signed it and gave me a comment of "Very good" and told me "Excellent." And afterward, I rudely told her that this was a greeting card and that I was doing it for our favorite mathematics matron, who was going to retire from our school. So, try to clear your things instead of someone else taking that thought differently and expressing it before you and you can't be rescued from it.

But I want to share one more thing with my readers. From school life or childhood life, I have not faced the spotlight and I was in the darkness, as I used to hide myself, my feelings, my talents, and anything related to me from people. I always used

    How to get out of an Unemployment Trap

to stand beside someone, like my friends, cousins, and others, and those people always live with the attitude that they are the greatest ones.

So, try to do well and do think well for yourself from childhood, so people will take you for granted. If you always do things in a joking way, they will always take your things as a joke only. And that's what happened to me in my life. So try to learn from my errors.

Commitment to Self-If you commit something to yourself, then it will reflect that seriousness. The very first thing you must do is talk to yourself and honestly share everything in your life. After that, you will better understand the things that matter most in life. Try to reach out to all your thoughts while you are alone or with your favorite people.

Some dedicated students or people are possessive enough to be punctual. So they try to create targets for themselves and put them on the Cabbort on Chart paper and also create a routine timetable to follow in a daily way with some seriousness. But what about lazy people? They complain that I took a book with excitement to read it, but I didn't complete it. Or some are like, they do create such timetables but are unable to follow them daily. But it's not like they are not serious about their career, goals, and success. They must discover their own life's purpose and commit to carrying it out. 'No,' instead, try new things, take knowledge, and work with it to determine whether the things are for your good or not. Try out your own time to wake up and practice harder with concentration to achieve that particular goal in life. Then you didn't require any moment to find out the things to work for your dream. Those are natural things that will happen automatically.

Try to keep some points in mind:

Don't repeat what your responsibilities are for the particular dream. I used to tell and recall myself every time I wanted to wake up and have to write a book, and the result was that I didn't feel the energy about doing something. Instead, I tried out the things that I wanted to help my unemployed friends, for which they would get some good vibes by reading my 'Unemployment Ability Book'.

2. I always didn't listen to anyone, and I also didn't follow it daily. So I tried to tell myself the reason behind doing the particular work, which is directly connected with an emotion, such as rejection and achievement. By doing this, I always find a smile on my face that the particular failure I faced in my life should not get wasted and also brings a smile on my face for two reasons. As my favourite teacher told me, always keep a smile on your face when you find any problems or are quite emotional and it will help you fight off that problem. I usually do those things, but while writing this book, sometimes I lost focus. Then I remembered the starting time and asked a question: "Why should I have started doing this work?" and a smile gave me the answer and I became more serious about writing a book.

3 Be limitless because if you have any limitations, you will only put in that much effort to accomplish that much. So try to avoid limitations. If someone keeps any limitation in a sports tournament, like in cricket, a 20-over match, and you want to do something in that much time, what will you do? I will try to give myself a target so that I will break the record of scores in it.

To achieve a particular goal, you will need to find a particular reason for it.

How to get out of an Unemployment Trap

Chapter- 10
REVOLUTIONARY

If you want to change something, first find out what needs to change in yourself.

But if you want to do something in life and no one believes in you, you must become the strongest person, capable of standing alone, walking alone, and moving from there alone. To achieve anything in life, you must first become a revolutionary for yourself.

First, tell yourself, "Let's do the specific work that makes you happy. "Because in our lives, some are the people who directly tell us what they think, what they want. They are extroverts. But those problems they face are those introverts who didn't have the freedom to do something in life on their own.

[Becoming ambitious is good, but it's not good that we can't be able to do anything for ourselves and our dreams.]

To Become a Revolutionary: There are some ways to create freedom for yourself.

1. Think well about yourself first.

2: Give your thoughts freely and speak in depth with your friends and cousins on a specific topic; even if you are wrong and do not have much knowledge to win the conversations, make it clear that you are right and you trust yourself.

3: For shy people Keep your mind away from toxic words and people because introverts think most about what affects their actions.

Make a list of what you want to do in life. And do it freely, which will help you to open up and to become stronger.

5: Don't keep your mouth shut because people think that they can easily dismiss you by emotional drama or by harshness.

6: Take a stand for yourself and don't try to explain.

If you did it, then no one will be there to take advantage of you, as it happens in ragging that someone is there who suffers the pace as he or she can't be bothered to stand and fight for their path. So don't hide your fear from anyone, and don't let anyone force you to use scary things.

Let's talk about the example. In a family, we are blessed with our cousins, but are you that sure that you are lucky to have such people in your life? In one family, there are three cousins and two parents who leave together. In the absence of their parents, two cousins who are older than the third person, who was the favourite child of their parents, never thought to shout at their smallest child, who was in 5th or 6th class, and their elders were in 10th or 9th class. So in the absence of the parents, the elders were free to show their powers to that little one, and, regardless of what happens, the child goes to their parents to share everything with them, and then their elderly one got the punishment from their parents. This has gone on for a few years.

But once they got the clue about the youngest cousin, their parents would not treat her as they had previously. So, then they started giving torture to the youngest one and told him not to tell anything to their parents, just follow what we want and keep us happy. This goes on for a few months, and 2 or 3 months is enough to damage the mind of the human body or give the problem of depression or anxiety. And this affected the studies of that girl too, and on the result day. When her parents asked for a report card, her swelling started and her voice was not coming out, but then she tried to write it down and tell her parents, and then she asked them if by beating them they would again think bad about her and if she wanted to have a good friendship with them.

So, guys, torture is a big curse and you don't need to give anyone freedom to make you punished, to make you tortured.

          How to get out of an Unemployment Trap

Try to keep clarity and don't need to make any rectifications about it. If you hide something, then people will make it their point to create damage for you. So don't give anyone reason to take revenge on you in any way.

Trust Yourself

If you have hidden anything, as your parents didn't trust you, that's a big loss, and you feel that you are doing something wrong, due to which your parents are also not happy with the decision. However, there will be times when you must make decisions that are best for you, and you will only gain a better understanding of them as time passes.

In a student's life, some students face this problem during their carrier path. A student wanted to go for science, and his personality did look like he would study well in it. But he wanted it badly. So what if he had to do it? Does personality matter most in life while choosing a career? His parents didn't think so either that he could be able to do it. Instead, they think that he can do it well by choosing commerce or the arts. His parents didn't have high expectations for him.

Sometimes it happened that when a student was serious regarding his career, his parents didn't show that much seriousness. So it is better to try to take your stand to achieve your life goals. So here you want to do the things that sometimes happen when we don't recognize what we want in life and also get confused by the four choices, so we take the wrong choice. So firstly, try to make simple choices about anything; try to give yourself time to make decisions; try to gain self-understanding about your likes and dislikes. Try to point out the reason behind choosing the particular option. Make the list and then check how many people are good at it. Then take the decision instead of asking the elders or counsellor about it.

Don't Run Away from the Problems: Try to understand the situation, not the people's words. If you run away from them, then they will create a high level of misunderstanding, due to which no one will trust you. At least try to fight for yourself, or at least take a stand for yourself.

One day I was doing office work and something mistakenly happened as I made one mistake in my content and it was uploaded on the company site. The mistake happened in the location where it was changed after editing, and before editing, I had written it was correct, so I did not recheck. That's a big mistake for me. I became vulgar to my senior after knowing that I had done something wrong in my work. She became vulgar to me and whatever she said, I wrote it on my not scribbled wall where I sit and work. And after that result is that I work well, and I think well about myself. People will judge me on this; I have listened to their rude behaviour and employees should not need to listen up. Instead, they will directly fire me. And it's also not like you changed after doing this, because what our seniors want from us is that we listen to their every word, whether it's bad or good. Let me tell you guys that whatever I have done is just because I wanted to do it. It's not like they were giving me the torture to work well.

First, you must determine the reason for your decision, as well as the reason for your movement or action. You must need to check out for yourself what is good and what is bad in life. Whether it's a particular thing, person, place, or anything else, try to keep those away from you, as these things only spread negativity in your mind and, due to that, your positivity will be hidden from your end. And always keep things straight to be understandable, and it will be more helpful when you tell the truth because half of the problems occurred. After all, we were afraid, to tell the truth to ourselves or our family due to their reactions, which caused us stress, and if our reason is good, then no one can stop us from doing something in life.

Do what you want to do.

Achieve what you want to.

But my friends, you must take a risk because in life without effort, no one achieves success. If you are sure that you want to do this, then you don't need to worry about its result. You will need to cross the obstacles and win the race.

If you understand and take guidance from your favourite person by sharing with him what you want to do, first try to convince your parents. If not, then move to them. If you didn't have any supportive parents, then take lessons from your life. For example, if you have done anything and failed, find out why you failed in it. What God wants to make you realize

Overcome your fear- If you want to become stronger then take out all the fears and sorrows. You will act emotionally, you will take your life decisions emotionally, and so on. You can't go away from it, as your people can't let you know that your choices were wrong, as they will think this way, they will get more benefits, and so on. No one can make you realize this instead of you.

1. Never make an emotional or angry decision.

Don't spoil the movement by stress; just live in the present.

3: Keep yourself happy so that you can make the best decision based on your happiness.

4 explore new things in life.

But it is not easy to handle or overcome your fear of failure in life. To begin, you must step outside of your comfort zone and try new things to improve your choices and lifestyle.

1 Make a list of your fears.

2 includes your qualities, good and bad, separately.

3: Include what you are and are not capable of doing.

4 any skill.

5 disabilities

6 what you want to do, where you want to go, what you want to eat, and so on.

The final step is to mark the fear that makes you nervous while dealing with it. For example, in my list, I have said I have a fear of heights, so after doing paragliding I must be able to overcome my little fear. Not fully, but little change I will surely get from it.

Mental health must be good.

We all have such a mental illness in mind. It's just that we only mentally stress about such things in life. We just need to throw out such stress from our lives, as Swami Vivekanand has said, "What you think about yourself, you do like it." As your mind gives movement to your body parts, in such a way, you only go through.

Your actions decide your success, but your mind will decide to take such an action.

Why do we take time? Why do we think that this is not the right time for our success? Because sometimes we think that we are not ready to do action or work or mentally we are not prepared as our mind is disturbed and due to stress, we think we should delay our work.

Give freedom to your thoughts. Give freedom to yourself.

Mental stress affects your actions.

Precautions to stay away from mental stress: -

1 Don't ever try to change your mind when you are not ready.

2 Don't you dare give anyone a chance or your life decision authority to anyone when you are not in good condition.

3. Don't try to hear more advice from people, which will increase your stress and anxiety.

4, Reach out to a private space, which could be a private cottage, a forest location, or something else. Keep one private

          How to get out of an Unemployment Trap

place for yourself to get some good vibes.

5. Maintain a positive attitude by listening to music, dancing, socializing with friends, and so on. Spend more time with your favourite squad.

6. Do meditation, yoga, and positive affirmations help people avoid stress?

7: Make time to talk to yourself and share everything you've done in the past year, especially what you've done for your dream since the day you realized it. What action do you need to take for your success?

8 Gain Clarity to Permit Actions and try to give yourself freedom.

CONCLUSION

In this whole book, I have not written or told anything about the employees who left the job after a short period just to get a hike, and why not? It's all their right to get what they deserve in the professional area.

The thing is to understand that an employee asks for a hike sometimes and then doesn't get his salary, which is insufficient for him. After keeping some patience, they didn't wait and took a move to another company, and this is the actual problem because there are two people (the employee and the corporate company, or you may say the platform where you get paid).

If you leave that job, which is in an MNC, the company will get a new trainee in the office because the new joiner will not reject the opportunity to work in an MNC, and this is the actual path where an employee's value is zero for that company as their demand can be fulfilled by anyone, but the employee needs to create his value in the office.

Why would a multinational corporation pay a higher salary to a middle-class employee? What are you doing that no one else can, or what distinction are you making in your work that will earn you more money?

All thanks to the lockdown by which we all have to deal with the real thing in our lives. And here we all have seen that during the lockdown, the corporate sectors have also built their strength in such a way that they aren't afraid of anything, even if an employee leaves the company or whatever.

So, we have to make an understanding between a company and an employee, which is the conclusion of this book on how to get out of an unemployment trap.

But how is this possible? The possibility arises according to the situation, and this can't be disclosed here because everyone faces different challenges in their life, but the solution is only one, which is to be positive and spread positivity everywhere and keep yourself financially stable.

 How to get out of an Unemployment Trap